Squirmy Wormy

by Lynda Farrington Wilson

Sensory World

an imprint of Future Horizons

Squirmy Wormy

All marketing and publishing rights guaranteed to and reserved by

1010 N Davis Dr.
Arlington, TX 76012
877-775-8968, 682-558-8941
682-558-8945 (fax)

info@sensoryworld.com
www.sensoryworld.com

ISBN 13: 978-1-935567-18-9

Dedication

For Joshua, Christopher and Tyler...
your brilliance of spirit and warmth of heart inspires
me each and every day, and to Richard, for helping me
to reach for and embrace the brass ring.

My name is Tyler. I have autism and SPD, or Sensory Processing Disorder. I am learning why I do some of the silly things I do and how I can help myself, or ask for help when I need it.

I CAN HELP MYSELF!

Sometimes I watch the ceiling fan go around and around, or spin the wheels on my cars...
SPIN, SPIN, SPIN, SPIN, SPIN

But what I really need is a long ride on the merry-go-round at the playground. A-a-h-h-h, much better.

I NEED THE PARK!

(or a Sit 'n Spin, or spinning on a swing, or a game of "Ring around the Rosie")

Sometimes I feel like I need to run really fast...
RUN, RUN, RUN, RUN, RUN
But what I really need is a s-q-u-e-e-z-e in the couch
cushions like a hot dog, to calm me down.

Whew, I feel better.
I NEED A SQUEEZE!
(or bear hugs, or carrying the laundry basket, or crashing onto my
bean bag, or rolling a big ball on my belly)

Sometimes when I watch TV, I can't help but stare at the words going up and down, and back and forth because I love seeing fast words fly by...

UP AND DOWN, UP AND DOWN, UP AND DOWN

But what I really need to do is bounce on my ball or jump on my trampoline. O-o-o-o-o-o-o, that feels better.

I NEED TO JUMP!

(Or make a game of pounding on the soles of my feet, or rocking in a rocking chair, or jumping on a pogo stick)

Sometimes my hands just don't behave, like they are two monsters that jump around, or hit or pinch...
FLAPPY, FLAPPY, PINCHY, PINCHY, HIT, HIT, HIT

8

Those two monsters really need to squeeze some clay or
dig in the sandbox or a bin full of dried beans...
there, there now, monsters.

I NEED QUIET HANDS!

(or fidget toys, or squeeze balls, or maybe I'm just frustrated and cannot
communicate exactly what I'm feeling)

Sometimes I feel like things are running around in my head so fast that they don't make sense...

VROOM, VROOM, VROOM, VROOM, VROOM!

But a good long swing makes me feel much better.
I NEED TO SWING!
(slow, calming swinging, or a massage with lotion on my feet, or deep-pressure hugs)

Sometimes in school I just can't seem to sit still in my chair,
like I have creepy crawlers in my clothes...

SQUIRMY WORMY,

SQUIRMY WORMY,

SQUIRMY WORMY.

So I ask the teacher for a break and I S-T-R-E-T-C-H really tall
and I take my squeezy toys or wiggly pen back to my seat and

SQUISH, SQUISH,
WIGGLE, WIGGLE.

Goodbye you squirmy wormy!

I NEED A BREAK!

(Or a lap pad, a weighted vest, a compression vest, a seat wedge, or just a drink of
water down the hall and a skip back to class)

Sometimes there are so many sounds in my ears that I can't understand what my teacher is saying because sounds that other people can ignore are really loud to me...

BANG, CLANG, YADDA-YEE, PSSSST, B-B-R-ING, CRUNCH, CLICK

And I know this is when I need a quiet-spot break to listen to my music or look at a book. H-u-s-h-h... that's better.

I NEED MY QUIET SPOT!

(or music with headphones, a small tent, a bean bag chair in the corner of the classroom, or a walk in a quiet hallway)

P-S-S-T
P-S-S-T

Sometimes I just get upset and confused and I don't know what else to do but scream or cry...

S-C-R-E-A-M, S-C-R-E-A-M, S-C-R-E-A-M

But I just close my eyes, take a deep breath and think of something that makes me happy.

IT'S OKAY WHEN I FEEL UPSET.
I WILL FEEL BETTER SOON.

Sometimes, even when I am tired, things keep racing through my head and I can't quiet my body down to fall asleep.
My arms and legs just feel like dancing...

DANCE, DANCE, DANCE,
DANCE, DANCE

So I ask my Mommy to
wrap me up in my blanket very snuggly,
rub my feet with lotion,
and give me really big hugs...

"Good night, my Mommy."

"Sweet, quiet dreams, my sweetheart."

I NEED SLEEP.

I CAN HELP MYSELF!

To learn more about SPD:

The SPD Foundation sponsors an online site with lots of information about sensory processing disorder. There are all types of community and healthcare resources for people with sensory problems, including dentists; physicians; occupational, physical and speech-language therapists; educators; mental health professionals; eye care professionals, and community resources, such as hair salons and gymnastics programs. The site is adding community resources, such as hair salons and gymnastics programs. If you know of resources in your area, please visit this website and add them to the list.

This site also includes a link to SPD Parent Connections, a nationwide network of parent-managed community support groups for families interested in sensory processing problems.
www.SPDfoundation.net

Carol Kranowitz has a website that includes many pages of equipment, supplies, and other resources to assist people with sensory processing disorder. It also includes links to other useful sites.
www.out-of-sync-child.com

S.I. Focus magazine is the first of its kind serving as an international resource to parents and professionals who want to stay informed about sensory integration and how to address sensory processing deficits. *S.I. Focus* provides quality information written by leading people in the field as well as parents with insight into the topic.
www.SIFocus.com

Sensory World, the publisher of this book, is an imprint of Future Horizons, the world's largest publisher exclusively devoted to resources for those interested in autism spectrum disorders, Asperger syndrome, and SPD. The company also sponsors national conferences for parents, teachers, therapists, and others interested in supporting those with ASD and SPD.
www.thesensoryworld.com

Additional Resources

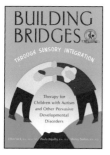

Aquilla, Paula, Yack, Ellen, & Sutton, Shirley. *Building Bridges through Sensory Integration,* 2nd ed. www.thesensoryworld.com

Arnwine, Bonnie (2005). *Starting Sensory Integration Therapy: Fun Activities that Won't Destroy Your Home or Classroom!* www.thesensoryworld.com

Lande, Aubrey & Wiz, Bob. *Songames™ for Sensory Integration* (CD). www.thesensoryworld.com

Fisch, Marla S. *Sensitive Sam: A Sensitive Story with a Happy Ending for Parents and Kids!* www.thesensoryworld.com

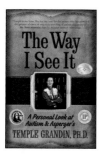

Grandin, Temple. *The Way I See It* and *Thinking in Pictures.* www.fhautism.com

Jereb, David, and Jereb, Kathy Koehler. *MoveAbout Activity Cards: Quick and Easy Sensory Activities to Help Children Refocus, Calm Down or Regain Energy.* www.thesensoryworld.com

Gray, Carol. *The New Social Story Book Illustrated.* www.fhautism.com

Koomar, Jane, PhD, Stacey Szklut, Carol Kranowitz, et al. *Answers to Questions Teachers Ask About Sensory Integration* (CD). www.thesensoryworld.com

Kranowitz, Carol. *The Out-of-Sync Child, 2nd ed.; The Out-of-Sync Child Has Fun, 2nd ed.; Preschool Sensory Scan for Educators (Preschool SENSE); Getting Kids in Sync* (DVD featuring the children of St. Columba's Nursery School); *The Out-of-Sync Child* (DVD); *Sensory Issues in Learning & Behavior* (DVD). www.thesensoryworld.com

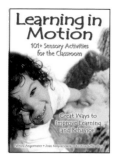

Krzyzanowski, Joan, Angermeier, Patricia, & Keller Moir, Kristina. *Learning in Motion: 101+ Fun Classroom Activities.* www.thesensoryworld.com

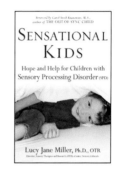

Miller, Lucy Jane, PhD. *Sensational Kids.* www.thesensoryworld.com

Moyes, Rebecca. *I Need Help With School! A Guide for Parents of Children with Autism & Asperger's Syndrome.* www.FHautism.com

Renke, Laurie, Renke, Jake, & Renke, Max. *I Like Birthdays... It's the Parties I'm Not Sure About!* www.thesensoryworld.com

These catalog companies can provide more ideas and products for kids with Special Needs.

Abilitations
(800) 850-8602
www.abilitations.com

FlagHouse Sensory Solution
(800) 265-6900
www.FlagHouse.com

Henry Occupational Therapy Services, Inc.
(888) 371-1204
www.ateachabout.com

Integrations
(800) 622-0638
www.integrationscatalog.com

Therapro, Inc.
(800) 257-5376
www.theraproducts.com